WALT DISNEY'S
Sleeping Beauty

ISBN 0 361 05867 5
Copyright © 1973, 1974, 1976 and 1983 Walt Disney Productions
Published 1983 by Purnell Books, Paulton, Bristol, BS18 5LQ,
a member of the BPCC group of companies.
Made and printed in Great Britain

The book Bambi is based on Bambi: Life in the Woods by Felix
Salten, translated by Whittaker Chambers, published by
Jonathan Cape Limited

Purnell

ONCE UPON A TIME a handsome king and his fair queen had a lovely baby daughter.

The child was called Aurora, which means The Dawn, and the day of her christening was proclaimed a holiday throughout the land. The happy King Stefan and his queen welcomed their many guests and the castle was gay with flags and waving banners. The courtyard swarmed with happy people.

Among the guests was King Hubert, who ruled over a nearby kingdom, and he brought his small son, Prince Philip, and the parents of the baby princess hoped that, one day, she would marry the young prince. "How splendid it will be," said King Stefan to King Hubert. "I am sure my daughter and your son will make a very happy pair! See how the boy's eyes shine as he looks at the baby!"

Of course Prince Philip did think that the little princess was very sweet but he had seen something else. Down a beam of sunlight he saw three small, bright creatures who flew with tiny fluttering wings.

Then came the voice of the major-domo of the castle. "Their most honoured and exalted excellencies, the three good fairies," he cried. "Mistress Flora, Mistress Fauna and Mistress Merryweather." And, as a trumpet sounded, the fairies curtsied to the king and queen. "Your majesties," said Flora in a clear, bell-like voice, "we have each come bearing a gift. Here is my gift!" And, waving her small wand over the cradle of the infant princess Aurora, she said: "Little princess, I give you the gift of beauty, the gold of sunshine in your hair, lips like roses and the springtime in your dancing feet."

Even as Prince Philip watched he saw a shower of sunbeams fall into the cradle from the tip of Fairy Flora's wand.

Then it was the turn of Fairy Fauna and she came forward to wave her wand and to cry: "Tiny princess, my gift is of song, of sweet melody your whole life long." And as she waved her tiny wand there came a shower of flower petals which floated down upon the cradle with a tiny, tinkling sound like fairy bells.

So Princess Aurora received two presents and it was the turn of Fairy Merryweather. Stepping forward, she said: "Sweet princess, my gift to you shall be . . ." But that was as far as she got. At that moment there came a howling wind that sent the great chandeliers swinging!

"What has happened?" gasped the worried queen.

"It is Maleficent!" gasped Fauna as there came a flash of lightning, a wisp of smoke and the wicked fairy.

"What can she want?" whispered Merryweather.

"Hush!" said Flora. "Listen! She is addressing the king."

"Well, King Stefan," the wicked fairy cried, "this is a fine gathering indeed. Why did I not receive an invitation?"

"I——" began the unhappy king.

"But," interrupted the wicked fairy, her eyes flashing fire, "since I am here I will bestow a gift on the child. Listen well, all of you!" Then, turning to the cradle, she stretched out her long arms.

"The princess," cried Maleficent, "shall indeed grow in grace and beauty. She shall be loved by all who know her. But before the sun sets on her sixteenth birthday she shall prick her finger on the spindle of a spinning wheel and——" The wicked fairy smiled evilly. "And DIE!" she finished.

"Oh no!" gasped the poor queen.

"Seize her!" roared the king, but, as the guards stepped forward to obey, Maleficent whirled round on them. "Stand back!" she screamed. There was a blinding flash of lightning, a clap of thunder and the bad fairy vanished from sight.

For a moment there was silence, then Fairy Merryweather stepped forward. "Do not despair, your majesties," she cried. "I can help even if I cannot undo this terrible curse." Then she spoke to the infant princess. "Sweet princess," she said, "if you should prick your finger you shall not die but fall into a magic sleep until the kiss of true love shall break the witch's cruel spell and you will awake!"

The other fairies were very pleased with what Fairy Merryweather had done but King Stefan was still very worried. "I must DO something," he cried. "I must have every spinning wheel in the kingdom burnt."

So it happened that, as night fell, a great fire was kindled in the central square of each town and village. And every spinning wheel in the kingdom was burnt. How the flames leapt and the wood of the spinning wheels crackled.

"Good, good!" said King Stefan. "I will beat the wicked fairy yet!"

But the three good fairies were not so easily satisfied.

"A bonfire won't stop Maleficent," said Merryweather. "I think I have an idea!" And she begged Flora and Fauna to listen carefully.

"There is one thing that the wicked fairy does

not understand," went on Merryweather, "and that is love and kindness."

"Yes, yes," put in Flora, "I see what you mean. WE must protect the princess

Aurora." And after a long talk the three good fairies arranged to bring up the little princess in a woodcutter's cottage. "But we must not use magic," went on Fairy Flora. "We must live like mortals for sixteen years. By doing that Maleficent will never suspect us. Come, let us tell the king and queen at once."

King Stefan and his queen listened very carefully to the plan, and because it seemed the best way to guard the baby princess from harm they agreed. So it happened that the king and queen parted from their little daughter and watched her vanish into the night with the three good fairies.

"Goodbye!" whispered the queen as she clung to her husband.

The years passed, as the years do, and they were not very happy years

for King Stefan and his queen. Yet at the woodcutter's cottage deep in the forest there was great happiness. There the baby princess grew into the loveliest of maidens and was known to her three fairy aunts as Briar Rose.

At last it was almost the day of Briar Rose's sixteenth birthday and the three good fairies, whom the sweet princess thought were her kind aunts, were very busy.

"Well," cried Briar Rose, as she burst into the parlour of the cottage, "what are you three dears doing?"

"Er—n-nothing!" said Merryweather quickly. Then she handed the girl a basket. "Please go to pick some berries," she said. "We need many more than you picked yesterday! Off with you!" And she hustled the rather puzzled maiden out of the room.

"Don't go too far," cried all three fairies, "and don't talk to any strangers!"

Briar Rose, who did not know that she was really the princess Aurora, promised to be careful and skipped happily away with her basket, leaving her aunts to decide to use their magic to make a cake and a lovely new gown for a birthday gift.

And that very day who should come riding along to meet the girl but none other than Prince Philip.

Of course the prince had no idea who the lovely maiden was. Yet he thought she was the most beautiful girl he had ever seen. "Who are you?" asked the prince. "What is your name?"

"My name is——" began Briar Rose. Then she remembered her aunts' warning. "Oh no," she cried, "I must not tell you. Goodbye!" And away she ran towards the woodcutter's cottage.

"Stop!" shouted the prince. "When will I see you again?"

"Never!" called back the girl. Then, because she could not bear to think she would never see the handsome young man again, she called out: "I will see you this evening —at the woodcutter's cottage!"

Meanwhile, great things were happening in the cottage. Having decided to use their magic to make a lovely birthday cake as well as a beautiful birthday gown, the three fairies scattered coloured magic in all directions. Little did they know that puffs of pink and blue magic were spouting from the cottage chimney as they waved their wands.

Suddenly Maleficent's pet raven, who had been sent to find the missing princess, happened to fly over the cottage. As soon as he saw that magic spouting from the chimney of the woodcutter's cottage he knew that his search had ended. "Where there is magic," he told himself, "there one can find fairies. Ho! Ho! Maleficent must learn about this!" And away he flew just as Briar Rose came tripping up to the cottage with a gay song on her lips.

"Oh!" cried the girl when she burst into the parlour and saw the birthday cake and the lovely birthday dress.

"Happy birthday, Briar Rose!" chorused the three good fairies.

"Sit down," said Fairy Flora; "we have something to tell you!" And, there and then, she told Briar Rose the truth about herself and how she was betrothed to Prince Philip.

"To-night, dear child," finished the fairy, "we are taking you to your father, King Stefan."

"No, no!" cried the poor girl. "I love another. I can never wed this prince of whom you speak!" And, sobbing, she ran out of the room.

Meanwhile Prince Philip was telling his father, King Hubert, that he could not marry the princess that had been chosen for him. "I have met a lovely girl, a peasant girl," he cried, "and I am going to marry her even if it means that I must give up my throne." And, without another word, he left his father's castle, mounted his favourite charger, Samson, and rode away towards the cottage in the woods.

Poor Prince Philip! As he rode towards the cottage home of the girl he had decided to marry she was being hurried to her father's castle by the three fairies. At last they reached Princess Aurora's own room. "In you go, dear," whispered Fairy Flora. "Make yourself comfortable while we find your father." And off they fluttered, leaving Briar Rose—or Princess Aurora as she should be called—sobbing in the dim and lonely dusk.

Suddenly a soft thread of music drifted into the young princess's room. It made her feel warm and comforted. As if under a spell the girl followed the melody which came from the fireplace. To her amazement

the back of the fireplace opened and there was a staircase leading into a lovely brightness.

Slowly Princess Aurora climbed the stairs.

Meanwhile Fairy Flora suddenly heard that melody. "Listen, listen!" she cried. "That is Maleficent's music."

"ROSE!" screamed Fauna and Merryweather. "Briar Rose! We must rescue her." And they raced back into the room. But it was too late. The girl had vanished.

"Quickly!" cried Flora. "We must break down the bricks that Maleficent has used to block up the staircase." But, although they used their

wands to make the bricks crumble, they were too late. Even as the three good fairies burst into a little tower room they saw Princess Aurora stretch out a slender hand to touch a spindle. Instantly her skin was pricked and the lovely girl crumpled to the floor.

"You poor simple fools!" came the laughing voice of the wicked fairy. "Did you think your stupid magic could defeat me? Well, there is your princess!" And, with an ugly laugh, she vanished in a puff of smoke.

So the wicked fairy's spell had come true after all. Even as King Stefan and his queen, as well as all the people of the kingdom, awaited the coming of Princess Aurora and Prince Philip, the girl was in a deep, deep sleep and the prince had walked into a trap set by Maleficent. Deep in the darkest dungeon of the wicked fairy's castle he sat chained to the stone wall with his head buried in his hands.

But the three good fairies were working hard to undo the evil that Maleficent had done. First they had put everyone in King Stefan's kingdom into a deep sleep. Then, fluttering as fast as their tiny wings would carry them, they hurried to rescue Prince Philip.

"Quickly!" they cried as they freed the young man. "Take this Sword of Truth and follow us!"

Freed from his dungeon and his chains, Prince Philip mounted Samson and galloped away, sparks flying from the gallant charger's hoofs.

In her throne room the wicked fairy heard the noise and knew what had happened. "Up with the drawbridge!" she screamed.

But her order was just too late. Prince Philip felt the drawbridge move under Samson's hoofs. "Jump, Samson!" he cried.

With a mighty leap the brave horse cleared a deep chasm to land safely on the other side. Not long afterwards he was slashing his way through a tangle of thorns that Maleficent had built around King Stefan's castle.

Slash! Slash! Philip carved his way through the thorn hedge towards the sleeping princess whom he now knew to be the girl he had met in the woods. Suddenly he saw a great dragon barring his way.

"Yes, it is I!" came the voice of Maleficent. "Now you will die!"

But with the Sword of Truth the brave prince put an end to the wicked fairy for ever.

With the three good fairies to guide him, Prince Philip climbed at last to the tower room where the sweet Princess Aurora lay sleeping. Slowly and tenderly he bent over her bed and kissed her.

Aaaaah! Through the sleeping castle and the whole kingdom went a sigh. It was a sigh of happiness

as everyone awoke to a new and beautiful day. All the troubles that had started when the wicked fairy came to the christening of the baby princess were forgotten. Instead, everyone was happy and gay and the wedding bells rang out in peal after peal.

"Don't they look happy," whispered Flora to Fauna and Merry-weather as the prince and princess appeared on the castle terrace and waved to the cheering people.

"Yes, yes!" chorused the other two good fairies. "May they be happy ever after!" And, as is the way with all fairy tales, Princess Aurora and Prince Philip lived happily ever after.

Walt Disney's
Lady
and the
Tramp

Lady was a cocker spaniel who came to live with two People called Darling and Jim Dear when she was a puppy.

It was a happy place to live, because Darling and Jim Dear were very fond of her, and provided her with two neat feeding bowls all of her very own. She had a round wicker basket too, lined with a soft, fluffy blanket, to curl up in when she felt a little tired or when she wanted to be left undisturbed.

Of course, it wasn't long before she had trained her People to feed her from the table – not with full meals, naturally, but with the very choicest titbits from their own plates.

Each morning she ran up the stairs with the morning paper, and most of the letters that the postman popped through the letter-box. And in the evening, when Jim Dear came home from work, he would whistle to her, and Lady would run to him, no matter what she was doing.

Lady felt that Darling and Jim Dear were the best kind of People to

have around the house. Jock and Trusty, two gentlemanly dogs who lived next door, agreed.

But there was another dog around the neighbourhood who had a few words to say on the subject – and he didn't agree with Lady, Jock and Trusty at all. Oh, no!

"I'll wear no man's collar!" he boasted. "No man is going to have me running little errands for him! I'm free – and that's the way I'm going to stay! Ah, this is the life!"

"But where do you sleep?" Lady asked him. "And who prepares your food? Can't you afford to keep a few People to look after these things for you?"

"It's quite a matter of choice, you know," replied The Tramp, airily. "If you know your way around – as I do – you can sort these matters out quite nicely without having to rely on People. Just wait, my proud beauty, until a baby comes to stay in your house! Things will be different then, I can assure you! There's only so much room for love in People's hearts. And when a baby comes, out goes the dog!"

Lady was very worried by these strange words. They worried her even more when a baby really did come to her house to live. Not that Darling and Jim Dear didn't mean to be kind, but what with all the bathing that the baby seemed to need, and all the meals in the middle

of the night, and so on, they were very busy. Lady remembered how, when she had been a puppy, she had needed extra attention. But this baby seemed to go on being a baby for such a long time, whereas her puppy days had been very short indeed.

And then a dreadful thing happened. Darling's Aunt Sarah came to visit. Aunt Sarah didn't like dogs.

"That creature must go out and live in the yard!" she said. "What's more, it should have a muzzle!"

Lady never thought that Darling or Jim Dear would take any notice, but she was wrong. The very next day Jim Dear fitted her with a nasty muzzle and tied her up in the yard. Lady yelped to Darling to do some-

thing about it, but it was no good.

It was awful being tied up in the yard, and the muzzle was so uncomfortable. Lady was so relieved when The Tramp came by, and wagged her tail furiously.

"Oho!" said The Tramp. "So it's happened already, has it, just as I said! Still, never mind. We'll soon get rid of that muzzle. Come along now."

"Come along?" cried Lady. "How can I? Surely you can see I'm tied up to this post?"

"Oh, *that*," said The Tramp, scornfully. "That's nothing. I forgot you don't know the first thing about doing anything for yourself. Look – watch me."

Lady watched as he showed her how to lunge against the rope until it broke. Then away they went, to get the muzzle off.

"You *are* clever," said Lady, as they walked through the town.

"It was nothing," said The Tramp. But he looked pleased, all the same.

"Where are we going?" asked Lady. "And how will we get the muzzle off?"

"Just to see a friend of mine," said The Tramp, at the entrance to the Zoo. "He lives here."

The Tramp's friend turned out to be Beaver, who looked pleased to see them.

"Hello, Beaver," said The Tramp. "Like to help us out?"

"Certainly," said Beaver. "Always glad to oblige, you know me. I say, Miss, that's a very fine muzzle you've got there."

"That's just what we want to get rid of," said The Tramp. "If you

can get it off, you're very welcome to keep it for your own use."

So Beaver chewed the muzzle off, and Lady and The Tramp left him trying it on.

"Where would you like to go?" asked The Tramp. "The world is wide. We'll go anywhere you like. A trip to the seaside, perhaps? Or a few days in the country?"

"Oh, I must go home," said Lady. "I've got to watch the house and baby, you know."

"What? After the way they've treated you?" replied The Tramp.

"I'll never understand women!"

But Lady was so determined about it that The Tramp gave in and they were soon in the street outside Lady's house.

"I'll peep in through the window, first, to see if there's anyone around," said Lady. "After all, I'm a yard dog now, you know."

The two dogs peered over the sill of the downstairs window, and The Tramp's nose twitched.

"Something wrong here," he growled. "And look, Lady – there's a

flicker of fire over there!"

Lady didn't wait a minute longer. She raced indoors – to save the baby, and Jim Dear and Darling!

The Tramp was right behind her as she dashed up the stairs, barking wildly. While she woke Jim Dear and Darling, The Tramp stood guard at the baby's crib. Just to show there was no ill feeling, Lady looked round for Aunt Sarah, but she seemed to have gone home.

Jim Dear and Darling were cross with Lady for causing all the noise, until they saw the fire. Then they were very thankful!

When the fire had been put out, Jim Dear took The Tramp to one side.

"Jolly good show you did there," he said. "I'd like to offer you a home and a job. What do you say?"

The Tramp remembered what he'd said about wearing no man's

collar, and sighed. Then he looked at Lady.

"Thank you, Sir – I'll take it!" he replied. He and Jim Dear shook paws.

It's a strange thing, but now Lady and The Tramp have *two* families to look after. Darling and Jim Dear and the baby are one.

But by far the most difficult task is to look after the other . . . a family of roly-poly puppies! But Lady thinks it's all quite worth it, and as for The Tramp – well, he's quite the proudest dog in town!

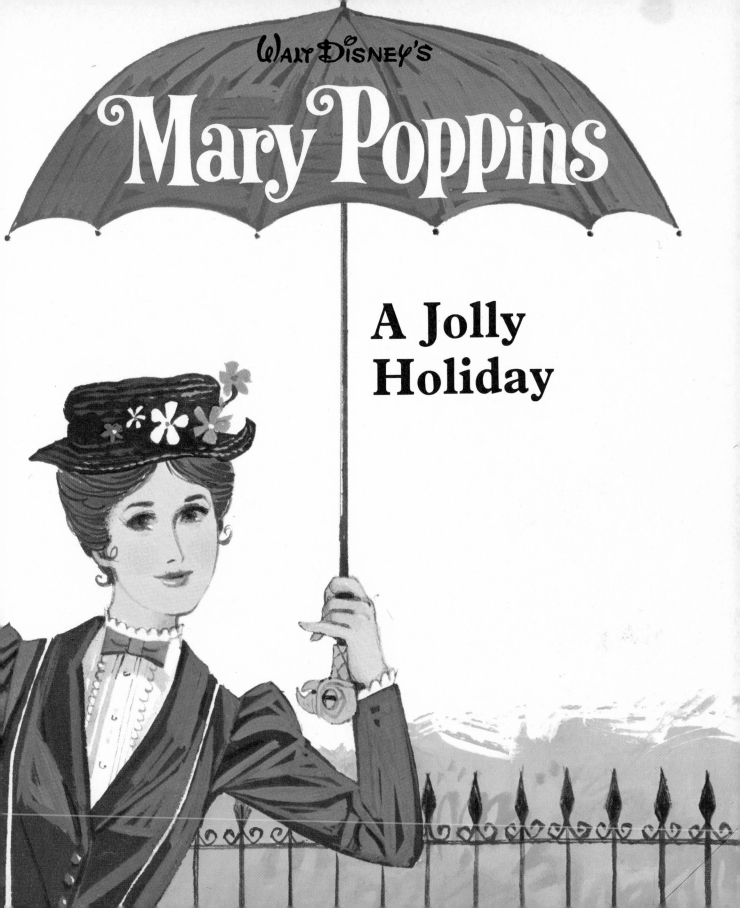

Mary Poppins, the new nanny, had just taught Jane and Michael Banks a game called "Well Begun is Half Done, or Tidy up the Nursery." It was such fun that when the game was over and the nursery was neat as a card of new pins, Michael wanted to do it all over again.

"Nonsense!" said Mary Poppins. "Spit-spot! Time for an outing in the park!" So Michael and Jane put on their hats and coats, and followed close on Mary Poppins' heels as she sped out through the gate and into Cherry Tree Lane.

Down the lane, Mary walked so quickly that Jane and Michael had to skip to keep up. But at the entrance to the park she stopped. For there was Bert, the jack-of-all-trades. He was down on his knees on the pavement, making pictures with coloured chalks.

The pictures were lovely. There was one of boats on the river. And another of a circus—not a very large circus, but still, there was a lion and a tiger and a man on a unicycle. Michael stopped to admire it. But Jane strolled on.

All at once she stopped too.

"Oh, this is a lovely one," she said. "I'd like to go there."

"An English countryside," said Bert with pardonable pride. "What's more, though you can't see it, there's a little country fair down that road and over the hill. Quite a suitable spot for travel and high adventure, I should say."

"May we go, Mary Poppins—please?" begged Michael.

"I have no intention," said Mary Poppins, "of making a spectacle of myself, thank you."

"Then," said Bert with a wink for Michael and Jane, "I'll do it myself."

"Do what?" asked Michael.

"Bit of magic," replied Bert taking each child by the hand.

"It's easy! You wink . . . you think . . . you do a double blink . . . you close your eyes and—jump!"

"Really!" sniffed Mary Poppins. But she put up her umbrella. And away they all went, straight into the English countryside.

It was a beautiful spot, green and quiet and sparkling with sun. Bert and Mary Poppins were dressed for the occasion. He was wearing an entirely new suit of clothes—and best of all, a new straw hat. She was dressed in the height of fashion, from her wide-brimmed bonnet down to the diamond buttons shining on her shoes. Jane and Michael looked just as elegant.

"And nothing makes a holiday complete," said Bert, "like a spot of afternoon tea."

He waved his arm, and there before them in an open place filled with sunlight stood a tea pavilion.

"Strike me pink!" said Mary Poppins. That was what she said when she was especially pleased.

Soon they were seated at the best table, with waiters hopping about to serve them.

"Now then," said Mary Poppins, studying the menu, "what would be nice? Some raspberry ice and cakes with icing—and tea?"

"Anything for you, Mary Poppins," said the waiter, who looked exactly like a penguin. "Order what you will, there will be no bill, it's com-pli-men-ta-ry."

When their tea was finished, Bert and Mary waltzed away; it was much too jolly a holiday to walk in the usual way. Down the road they went to the merry-go-round.

The merry-go-round slowed down as they approached it. They leapt aboard, landing gracefully on the horses' backs. Jane and Michael were very pleased to see them.

"Imagine!" cried Jane. "Our own private merry-go-round. Oh, this is such fun!"

"Very nice," said Bert, putting on a fine air, "very nice indeed— that is, if you don't want to go anywhere."

"Who says we're not going anywhere?" cried Mary Poppins with a toss of her head. And she had a word with the guard.

"Right-ho, Mary Poppins!" he smiled, and he lifted his cap. Then he pulled the tallest lever on the merry-go-round machine—and off went the horses galloping across the countryside.

In the distance a hunting horn sounded.

"Follow me!" called Mary Poppins over her shoulder. And away they rode to the call of the horn, passing huntsmen and hounds alike. As they galloped on, Bert even reached down and scooped up the fox for a ride.

They were now travelling so fast that the children scarcely noticed that Mary Poppins had left their side.

Suddenly, Mary Poppins was in the middle of a horse race. And being Mary Poppins, she won.

As she received congratulations on her splendid victory, the first raindrops fell.

There was a flash of lightning, then a sudden downpour.

They all huddled close under Mary Poppins' umbrella, while all around the countryside seemed to run together. Mary Poppins' pretty bonnet melted, and the diamonds vanished from the buttons on her shoes.

Jane and Michael looked politely away . . . why, there was the park! They were standing on the pavement just around the corner from Cherry Tree Lane. And on the paving stones, Bert's drawings were melting into bright puddles of rain.

"Oh Bert," said Mary Poppins, "all your fine drawings . . ."

"There are more where they came from, Mary my dear," said Bert. And he smiled at her, as if in his eyes she still wore the lovely bonnet and fine clothes and the diamond buttons on her shoes.

"Hurry along, children," said Mary Poppins. "Spit-spot or we shall be late for supper. Good-bye, Bert."

And she smiled at him. She was still smiling, was Mary Poppins, when they turned into Cherry Tree Lane . . .

Soon the children and Mary Poppins were snug in the nursery once more, with a fire glowing in the fireplace. On the hearth stood three pairs of shoes, drying out from the dash through the rain. Beside them leant Mary Poppins' umbrella. The parrot on its handle was blinking sleepily.

Supper was over, and Mary Poppins was tucking Jane and Michael into bed.

"I shall never be able to sleep," said Jane. "So many lovely things have happened today."

"I beg your pardon?" said Mary Poppins.

"Why, when we rode on the merry-go-round," said Jane with a yawn. "And the horses jumped off and raced across the countryside," Michael broke in. "And you won the big race, Mary Poppins!"

"A respectable person like me," gasped Mary. "In a horse race? What a suggestion!"

"But it did happen!" Michael insisted, sitting straight up in bed. "I saw it! And I don't *want* to go to sleep."

"Very well," said Mary Poppins. "Suit yourselves." She sat in her rocking chair and began softly to sing:
"Stay awake, don't rest your head,
Don't lie down upon your bed.
While the moon drifts in the skies,
Stay awake, don't close your eyes."

But Jane and Michael did not hear her. For they were fast asleep.

One spring morning in the forest there was such a hustle and bustle among the animals! The reason for all the commotion was really very simple. In a sheltered glade in the middle of the thickets a tiny prince had been born. All the rabbit family went to see what the new baby looked like.

"I'm used to new babies—I have a lot of them myself," said Mrs. Rabbit to the new arrival's mother. "But your child is something very special, I must admit. It's not every day one gets to see a baby deer."

"That's because we're rather shy creatures," said the deer, licking her baby's ears gently. "I'm glad you like him. His name is Bambi."

"Bambi, is it?" screeched the owl from a branch high above their heads. "He looks even more of a sleepyhead than I am! Come on, young fellow-me-lad, wake up and look around you! Haroo, haroo!"

When the owl made his awful screech even the rabbits jumped. Bambi sneezed and suddenly gave a great big yawn.

"My goodness, that's very rude of him!" thought one of the rabbit children. "Doesn't he know that he should put his paw over his mouth when he yawns?" Bambi didn't know that. But then he was only a very young fawn and didn't know any better. Good manners would come later!

Every day Bambi grew a little bit more, and one day he decided that he would like to explore the forest where he lived. So he bounded away down the trail by the edge of the stream, sniffing the air and thinking what a lovely day it was. And then he came upon a family of quail, out for a breath of morning air.

"Dear me, sir, you quite startled me!" said Mrs. Quail. "Now line up, children, and say good morning to the fine gentleman!" And all six children did exactly as they were told!

Then Bambi bounced away along the trail until a most peculiar sight caught his eye.

There, hanging from a tree branch, were three little animals!

"Hello!" said Bambi in a friendly sort of way. But the creatures didn't answer him.

"Perhaps they didn't hear me," thought Bambi. So he bent down and twisted his head round so that he could look at their faces the right way up. Then he saw that they were asleep.

"What a funny way to go to sleep!" thought Bambi. He wanted to laugh, but he was afraid that if he did he would wake them up.

"Boo!" said a little voice behind him, and Bambi turned round to see that one of the young rabbits who had come to visit him when he was only just born was standing there. "They are funny creatures aren't they? You'd think they were mice if you didn't know any better," the rabbit said.

"Please, I don't know what mice are," said Bambi.

"Really? Don't you know anything?" said the rabbit in surprise. "You're a lot bigger than me, even if you are so young, but you haven't learned very much yet, have you?"

"No, but I'm learning things all the time," said Bambi. "Would you like to help me?"

The rabbit felt very proud.

"Me . . . help a prince of the forest?" he said. "What an honour! Thank you very much, I'd be delighted to teach you what I know."

So Bambi and the young rabbit, whose name was Thumper, walked on together through the forest. As they walked, Thumper pointed out the flowers to Bambi, and showed him the birds flying over their heads.

"Now do you know what a bird is?" he asked. Bambi nodded.

"That's a bird!" he cried, sniffing at a beautiful coloured creature which had alighted on a log of wood nearby.

"No it isn't, silly!" said Thumper. "That's a butterfly!"

"Dear me," said Bambi. "There seems so much for me to learn."

"You're doing very well, really," said Thumper, feeling sorry for him. "And it was an easy mistake to make. After all, both butterflies and birds have wings, don't they?"

"What are wings?" asked Bambi. So the rabbit had to explain what they were, and how they were used.

"That sounds lovely," said Bambi. "Will I grow some wings one day?"

"No," said Thumper, patiently. "Whoever heard of a flying deer!"

Bambi thought a flying deer would be quite a lovely sight, but he didn't want the rabbit to think he was being silly, so he didn't say anything else. Instead, he chased the butterfly as it fluttered among the trees in the little glade.

All at once it landed on a pretty pink flower. And the flower shook! Bambi watched in amazement as the flower shook again. Then, from underneath the flower, someone said: "Atishoo!" And up stood a little black and white creature with the most amazingly large eyes.

"You're a flower?" asked Bambi, puzzled.

Thumper shrieked with laughter.

"That's not a flower, that's a skunk!" he said. "Flowers smell sweet, but skunks don't!" And he laughed all over again.

"I think it was lovely of you to call me a flower," said the skunk, smiling at Bambi. "I can see you're a very polite, well-brought-up sort of person. Really, you are the nicest person I've met for a long time."

"Thank you," said Bambi. "I *am* making a lot of friends this morning, and learning a lot of interesting things!"

Before very long Bambi knew everyone in the forest, and

everyone knew him. Then one morning he woke up to find another new experience awaiting him. Big drops of water were falling on him!

"Ooh, I don't like this!" he said to his mother. "Something cold and wet keeps hitting me!"

"It's only raining, little Bambi," said his mother. "If it didn't rain sometimes, the pool in the forest and the little stream over there would dry up and we would have nothing to drink."

Bambi wasn't the only one who didn't like the rain. In their nest, the little birds huddled together to keep warm. Mrs. Bird tucked as many of the babies under her wings as she could, but there wasn't room for all of them.

"Whee! This is fun!" said one of the baby birds. "Mummy, do you think that I could learn to swim like the ducks? They're birds too, aren't they?"

"They're not our sort of bird," said his mother. "Nobody in our family has ever done anything like that, and I hope you aren't going to be the first. Now snuggle down and try to keep warm, or you'll catch a very nasty cold!"

"Wake up, Bambi!" It was the next day and Bambi's friend, Thumper, had come to call on him.

"There are lots more things for you to see!" said Thumper as Bambi jumped to his feet. "Do you remember how cold and wet it felt when the rain fell yesterday?"

"Yes, I do!" said Bambi.

"Well, today you are going to meet a creature who actually likes living in water!" said Thumper. "Come with me!"

So Bambi scampered off to see who this funny creature could be. On the way they stopped for a quick snack in the clover bed.

"Only badly-brought-up rabbits eat the flowers and leave the leaves," said Thumper.

"Then why are you only eating the flowers?" asked Bambi.

"Because they taste nicer!" laughed Thumper.

Suddenly a little green creature jumped out beside Bambi.

"Oh! Who was that?" asked Bambi.

"That was Mr. Frog," said Thumper. "He lives in the water."

"In the water?" said Bambi, who was very surprised. "What a funny place to live!"

So Thumper took him to the pool and let him peer into the water.

"Why, there's another Bambi in there!" cried the little fawn.

"Silly!" said Thumper. "It's not another fawn, it's your own reflection!"

When winter came, Bambi was able to see the pool looking very different. For the surface had become hard and glassy instead of rippling and twinkling in the sunlight.

"That's called ice!" explained his friend, Thumper.

"It's so hard that you can walk on it!" So Bambi took some careful steps into the snow at the edge of the pool.

"Why, you're right!" he said, as he stood on the icy surface.

"What a clever rabbit you are!"

But the rabbit was chuckling. He ran out on to the ice behind Bambi and gave him such a big push that Bambi sat down fast and skidded along the ice.

"Oh!" cried Bambi.

"Don't cry—it's fun! said Thumper. "Snow and ice are very exciting things. Just watch me!" And he slid all the way across the pool.

"My legs get in the way when I try to do that," said Bambi, when he had tried to slide across the ice once or twice.

"Sit down, and I'll give you a push," said Thumper. So Bambi sat on the ice and the rabbit pushed him right across the pool. Because he had been expecting it this time, Bambi really liked the feeling of gliding across the ice.

"Now we'll try sliding in the snow!" said Thumper.

Soon he was rolling over and over in the snow beside the pool.

"Let's climb to the top of the hill and roll down again!" suggested Bambi. So they began to climb up the steep hill.

"Oh, wait for me!" cried Thumper before very long. "My little legs are sinking into the deep snow!"

When the two animals were out of breath from rolling down the hill and climbing back again, they looked for something else to do.

"Why, there's a hollow tree over there," said Thumper.

"What is a hollow tree?" asked Bambi. "Is it anything to do with holly?"

"No, it just means that it has died inside and is just a shell," said Thumper.

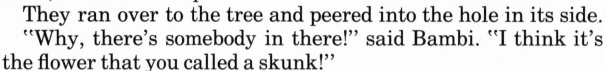

They ran over to the tree and peered into the hole in its side.

"Why, there's somebody in there!" said Bambi. "I think it's the flower that you called a skunk!"

"You mean the skunk that you called a flower," said Thumper.

"I like the name flower better," said Bambi. "Hey, Flower! Wake up!" The skunk rolled over and opened one eye.

"Oh, it's nice to see you, but please don't disturb me just now," he said. "Don't you know that we skunks—I mean flowers—have the habit of sleeping all through the winter?"

"That's true!" said Thumper. "I'd forgotten that!" And while Flower turned over and went back to sleep, he told Bambi all about the creatures which sleep all through the winter and only wake up in the spring.

At last the morning came when everyone in the forest knew that spring had come back to the earth. The birds knew it first, because they slept in the trees where the blossom sprouted on the branches. They whispered to each other, just to make sure it was true, and then they shouted from the treetops, "Spring is here! Spring is here!"

"Do you think that funny little fawn they call Bambi will be coming this way today?" said one bird to another.

"You mustn't call him a funny little fawn!" said the other bird, jumping up and down in excitement. "He'll be a proper prince now! He's lived in the forest for a whole year and he's on his way to being a stag!"

And so the forest knew that Bambi had grown up.